Who Killed Lilly Anne

Short Stories

James McEwan

Published March 2025
By Alibrasphere
Independent Publishing

British Library Catalogue-in-Publication Data.
A CIP catalogue record for this book is available from the British Library.
Paperback ISBN 13: 978-1-913202-02-6
eBook ISBN 13: 978-1-913202-22-4

Contents

Lilly-Anne

When I heard the front door close, I dashed to the window. From behind the lace curtain, I watched Lilly-Anne skip down the steps onto the street. Palpitations fluttered in my chest and my arrhythmia raced like a motor-cross Kawasaki skidding sideways across the sand.

She walked along the street wearing black low-heeled shoes, light blue stockings and her coat flapped with each step, exposing her knees. A handbag hung over a shoulder. Her lips glistened with a clear gloss on a pale face. She looked ill. I groaned. Perhaps her boss will give her the day off. I wished. She made her way along the road and disappeared from my view.

I sat down and began my breathing mantra; in for five seconds and out for five until I calmed myself sufficiently to let the pulsating surge in my groin subside. My hands no longer shook, and I could pick up my coffee.

Lilly-Anne had moved into the apartment block a few months ago, and since the day I accidentally brushed against her on the stairs, I have become an obsessive wreck. She had nodded a hello and smiled. A connection, with a mutual understanding that often telepathically passes between lovers, but she wasn't my lover, just an adorable stranger. When I stared into her grey eyes, an emotional detonation in my heart blasted a wave of blood to the surface of my skin. She stood still for a moment and had said, I'm Lilly-Anne. Paralysed, I didn't respond. She turned and ran up to her landing. The rear view of her firm body stirred a flush of lust through me, and my legs trembled. From then on, with her image imprinted in my mind, she controlled my thoughts and stimulated my dreams like a succubus that prowled through my night-time trances of sweats and stains.

All I need to do is speak to her. Perhaps a casual introduction with a gentle smile and ask her about the type of coffee she drinks. So, there I stood outside her flat engulfed in a warm air of percolated Arabic wafting beneath the door, like a hypnotic aromatic mixture of wood smoke and chocolate. This was my moment of courage ready to knock, just to say welcome to the block, but then my heart rumbled out of control and my practised preamble evaporated. My mind went blank, a numbness and a tingle crept up my legs, and I muffled a scream. Dragging my momentarily dead left foot, I turned and loped like the hunchback of Notre-Dame down into my hallway of loneliness. There I punched and kicked at my full-sized grizzly bear. Oh! how that seemed better. Sometimes, I think if it wasn't for my physical release of frustration on this stuffed monstrosity, I would go insane.

On another occasion, I came home early from work and paced my front room, back and forth. Through the window, I saw her arrive later than usual. I rushed into the front hall and stood waiting. I listened for her coming up the steps. Quickly, I pulled the door open and stepped out, intending to bump into her.

Her speed and agility surprised me. She side-stepped and said, sorry. Her eyes were tearful and red from crying.

Before I could reply, what was I going to say? She ran past and up the stairs. I followed to console her, but on the third step, I stopped. A relationship based on me taken advantage of her in a vulnerable and fragile state. No, I am better than that.

Back in my flat, I imagined the tattered bear flinch in response to my frustrated moan. I kicked its leg.

Sometime ago, I followed Lilly-Anne to her workplace. I needed to know what she did and discover something to talk about as an icebreaker. Standing outside the estate agent's window on the pretence of browsing the property advertisements, I watched her. She seemed agitated at her desk. There was a man perched on its edge. I crouched down to avoid being noticed and stared at her legs. I glimpsed pink panties, then saw my reflection in the window.

Lilly-Anne looked up at me and I panicked. My disguise was awful, dark glasses and a moustache. Did I look like a perverted creep? I rushed away up the road. She couldn't have recognised me, could she?

Who was the man following behind me? I dodged into a bookshop and waited until he passed. The staff at the till stared as I tore off the moustache. I sensed the strike of their thoughts, like a volley of darts from their eyes. Yes, I might be a creep. I tell myself I am normal. Is this what they mean by being besotted, irrational, and idiotic? Stalking is an offence, I know, I know! Am I depraved?

Friday evening after work, my colleagues insisted I come along to celebrate our team's success, a killing on the foreign exchange market. I had sweated all afternoon in the electrified excitement of fast money deals and swam immersed in an atmosphere of high-octane testosterone swirling in the office. It was like having my face caressed by a crotch as my palpitations raged back and forth. Yes, I needed a drink.

After my third tequila and grapefruit chaser, I saw her. Lilly-Anne sat at a corner table in the Saracen's Head. The man in a suite had his hand on her knee. She held his arm in a tight grip around its wrist. They looked tense. I took another swig of tequila for courage. I was going to say hello and get a conversation going. Too late. They got up and hurried out. My demeanour changed, and I slumped back in my chair as the thought thudded home. She had a man! Disappointed and saddened, I walked out, ignoring the calls from my colleagues to stay. Someone muttered, she's a wimp.

In the street with the fresh evening air, I sensed the alcohol pump through my veins. The effect surged my mood towards bravado. I would take a chance and pick up in Georgios, although I might hate myself in the morning. Who cares?

Alice was in her early twenties, with a half-shaved scalp and multicolour hair hanging to one side. Dressed in a Ben Sherman shirt, with pink braces holding up her stone-washed jeans, turned up to show off the bovver boots laced with yellow cord. Her youthful face was fresh, confident, and alert. A silver stud through her tongue flicked when she spoke. I smiled, and she joined me for some draft pilsner. We laughed.

She wanted to see my stuffed brown bear, so I invited her back. She stroked its nose. I caressed her cheek, and she stuck her studded tongue in my mouth. We were rough. She squealed in orgasmic ecstasy as she massaged my breasts and slurped over my nipples. Delighted, she squirmed and shimmered around in my bed.

In the early hours, she dressed to leave, but wanted to see me again, so I gave her a random business card that someone had slipped into my pocket at a meeting. I insisted she take a twenty-pound note for the taxi. After a limp wave, I closed the door.

Alice's Y fronts were lying in the bathroom, and I wondered where she had been the previous evening. In the shower, I gelled my body to cleanse away the stink of our female animal lust, which made me cringe as a wave of self-disgust shuddered through me. Where was the certainty in my life, with a commitment to a fulfilling future? It was a steady relationship I craved with Lilly-Anne.

It was a week later on a cool evening, as I walked home from work. The exercise was refreshing and gave me time to think. Where was my routine life going?

A car pulled onto the pavement in front of me. Shouting and screaming, Lilly-Anne got out and slammed the door. The driver blasted his horn.

"Can I walk with you?" she said and grabbed my arm. Her eyes were wet, and her face flushed an angry red.

I controlled my breathing, and forced my pulse to remain calm. Was I in heaven?

There was a rant of profanities from the driver in the car as he followed us until we dashed down a pedestrian only alley. I asked who the prat was.

Although it seemed perverse, the predicament was an opportunity for me and a moment of sheer delight, walking with Lilly-Anne.

I expected her to burst out with a flurry of excited reasoning, an explanation for her bust up. We walked on, and the silence was like a drum roll of reverberating agony in my head.

In the hall, I held her hand and asked if she was alright. She could come in for a coffee, just chat, maybe feel better, calm down. I was rambling. She said, give her a moment and then come up, and it would be nice to have some company.

In my flat, I kissed the bear. My grandfather had shot the poor creature for just being a bear and a trophy. I abused it as a punch bag to release my frustrations, yet for the first time, I kissed the ugly brute. Are there no limits to such cruelty?

Lilly-Anne sat on her settee. We drank strong black coffee, and she unloaded her story of abuse, harassment, and violence at work, of the persistent slow drip from a creepy pervert. He was Lilly-Anne's boss at the estate agency, a despicable creature. She told him she preferred women, but that didn't discourage his approaches. My heart skipped a few beats. He offered her a pay rise. He wanted to promote her. There was an opening in the office, provided, he had whispered; if she opened for him.

I listened with complete concentration, falling in love with the contours of her cheekbones, the soft rapid, lyrical voice, the way she would sweep loose hair away to one side. Vivid images of washing her back in the shower, brushing her auburn hair, and kissing her lips as I explored the soft crevices of her body. My heart was racing.

In the occasional break from her outpouring, as she sipped her coffee, I offered to help write and make her case to the company head office, to demand a change, and find a new position for her elsewhere.

For two weeks, she would come home sometimes smiling, but mostly crying and upset. We sat drinking coffee, and I would transcribe her harassment. I even suggested an industrial tribunal and compensation. She laughed and said I was going too far. Next day, I posted the letter.

We went to the cinema, and she cried all the way through *Bridget Jones's Diary*. Her words, filled with warmth and understanding, made me feel like I was floating on air. We kissed on her sofa until I broke off, since my palpitations and arrhythmia were racing beyond control.

A few days later, she called me at work and asked to meet in Costa's at lunchtime. She was giggling like a two-year-old on a sugar rush.

A top manager had come to the agency and offered Lilly-Anne a post with a pay increase in the central office. He sent her home to have a few days off work. The manager took her boss into the back office. I delighted in her success. She bubbled and purred over her café-latte as crumbs from a muffin dusted her chin. We walked along the canal path holding hands until I had to go back to work. I promised to cook a celebration dinner.

The first thing I did when I got home was to move my delightful bear from the hall into the broom cupboard. I wouldn't be needing him for a while. In fact, I might just find it a new home.

My favourite meal was chicken schnitzel, and rice, also I prepared a salad and warmed some bread rolls. I opened a bottle of red Gallo to let it breathe. My grandmother's Victorian dinner service would impress Lilly-Anne, and I covered the table with a white cotton cloth. Tonight, Lilly-Anne would learn of my emotions towards her, yes tonight I was ready.

The doorbell rang. I took a moment to calm my breathing, then walked with an air of confidence.

He stood there with a matter of fact, bland expression, and held up an identification card. Beside him were two pale-faced policewomen.

"I'm Detective Inspector McLean."

My stomach somersaulted and I gripped onto the door.

"Nothing to worry about," he said. "We are interest in the movements of a young woman. Do you know Miss Lilly-Anne Hawkins?"

I invited them in and sat at the table.

He told me they found Lilly-Anne's beaten body floating in the canal at fifteen-twenty hours that afternoon. How well did I know her?

My heart thudded, I began shaking, and I knocked over the wine, its ruby liquid soaked into the tablecloth and dripped in drops like blood over the floor. I burst into tears and began wailing as palpitations kicked at my rib cage. I was a lunatic heading for the madhouse.

My spirit left my body and looked down at me, shuddering in grief. What was I going to do now? My love in shatters, my dreams dashed. I became distant and disjointed, like an observer after a disaster. I was a hysterical woman slumped on the table. No longer normal.

Could I ever be normal? I had written the letter with meticulous detail, delighted to help my Lilly-Anne escape her abuse. She had signed it with a flourish. We had laughed.

I heard myself howling like a distant wolf. I had penned Lilly-Anne's death warrant.

"Miss Fletcher," the Inspector said, he pressed on the bridge of his nose. "I'll leave you with Jean and..."

"Caroline," a policewoman said.

"Yes, Jean and Caroline will look after you. Whenever you are ready, Miss Fletcher." He nodded to them. "They will take a statement." He spun away and strode out of the flat.

Forked Tongue

A creeping realisation of an inevitable disappointment replaced my expectations and excitement. I glanced around, searching the faces of people who rushed along the pavement. It was late. She wasn't coming. We agreed to meet here at half-past six, and in my jacket pocket I had five hundred euros in fifties. It was the last payment for an oil painting, a piece of art I found hypnotic. The scene depicted a battle of female sexuality and a vision of erotic conjecture. Although enthralled, I now felt a pang of regret for making this compulsive purchase. Last night, I paid a deposit of three hundred euros.

A waitress was clearing the opposite table, and she looked up at me. I was fidgeting with my napkin. She smiled, and I gave a brief nod in acknowledgement.

She came across with the tray. 'Noch einen Kaffee?' she said and collected up the two empty cups.

'No thanks,' I said and folded the napkin. 'I'll have a beer instead. Bitte.'

'Of course, ein Bier.' She wiped the table with a damp cloth. 'Ich komme gleich wieder,' she said and left.

I sipped the cool beer and sat back, accepting she had conned me out of buying a painting and all because of my inept skill at bargaining in the presence of a professional. I laughed out loud. The barman stared at me for a moment.

Was it possible that the three hundred euros was the price of her company? A charming temptress who magically lured me into her bed. Although, I was willing manipulated while in a hazy trance of heightened, lustful desires. Yet, all the time, transfixed on the idea of owning a unique piece of art and was oblivious to her slick manoeuvring. She was a beautiful woman, intelligent and articulate, with soft, sultry eyes.

I had arrived in Berlin last week, and yesterday I relaxed by having a coffee in this open-air café on the Ku-dam. I stirred my latte macchiato and absorbed the atmosphere of the street bustle while enjoying the warmth of the afternoon sun. A violinist in 17th century period custom, complete with a chalked wig, meandered around the tables playing the tune to *Three Blind Mice*. Some elderly ladies were clapping along with the music, and oblivious to the yellow petals from the linden tree drifting down onto the frothy cream in their cups and into their schnapps' glasses on the table.

'Ist hier noch ein Platz frei?' A woman stood by my table, shading her face from the sunlight.

'No. Please. Bitte sitzen Sie,' I blurted out, startled, as she had approached me from behind.

Moving around the table, she pulled out a chair. Still standing, she waved for service before she sat down in the shade.

A young girl in a starched white blouse with 'Café Kempinski' embroidered in gold letters on her chest pocket came and took her order.

I watched as the woman rummaged in her handbag and then placed it on the ground by her feet. She looked up at me. I looked away.

'Are you English?' she said and sat back in her chair.

'No, I'm,' I sat up from my slouch. 'No, I'm from Scotland.' I noted her olive complexion, firm cheeks, and black hair tied in a ponytail.

'Scotland!' she shouted, 'Schotte!' She leaned forward on the table and lowered her voice. 'You know, we Berliners know about your reputation for tight money and whisky.' She laughed. 'We say in German, die Schotten sind geizig mit ihrem Geld.'

'It's not true,' I said. 'Don't believe that. We aren't all so tight with our money.' I watched as she narrowed her eyes, pursed her lips, then shrugged, and gave a slight nod.

'We Berliners think it is true,' she stated.

The waitress placed her order on the table; apple torte topped with a peak of thick cream, a glass of corn schnapps and an expresso coffee, with an amaretto biscuit.

She lifted the fork and leaned forward to eat, and the top of her mauve silk blouse opened. I stared at her semi-exposed cleavage. A tattoo snaked up toward her shoulder beneath her blouse.

'Do you like apple torte?'

'Are you from Berlin?' I looked up into her face and saw she was grinning. I was flustered at being caught staring. 'It's just that I would guess you were perhaps Italian.'

'Italian!'

'Your complexion and hair, maybe Mediterranean.' I reached for my latte macchiato to avoid direct eye contact. 'I mean, your hair is nice. It's lovely.' I looked back, placing my cup on the saucer.

'Thank you.' She puckered her lips towards me, then she smiled.

'I always thought most German women,' I said and looking across at the group of ladies. 'Have blond hair—'

'And big bosoms,' she interrupted. 'All you Englishmen think the same.' She smirked.

'Scottish.'

'Oh yes, Schotte. No, I am from Berlin.' With her napkin, she wiped some crumbs sticking to her lips. 'My family is descendant from the Huguenots of France. We speak French, German and some Russian. My sister is married to a Greek who was born in Berlin. I also have an uncle. He lives in the Ukraine.'

'And your English is excellent.'

'Are you a tourist?' She lifted her schnapps glass and took a sip.

'No, I've been here a week, ready to start a new job.'

She moved her chair sideways towards the sun's rays shining through the branches of the tree and leaned back. Pulling her skirt up slightly, she exposed her bare thighs to the sunshine. I noticed a tattoo spiral around her upper leg and reach under her lingerie. I looked away.

There was a sudden screech that shuddered me, and I sat up with a jolt.

The violinist, directly behind me, played the tune *"That's Amore"*. In unison, the group of ladies sung along, "When the moon…hits your eye… like a big…pizza pie…that's Amore."

I took some coins out of my pocket and pushed them into the violinist's leather cup on his belt. I waved him away. Groans came from the ladies, followed by a few tut tuts and they shook their heads towards me.

'Das is aber Schade!' I heard someone say. 'Sie sind schönes Liebespaar.' The group all nodded together. They called to the violinist to come over to their table and reached for more schnapps.

'German ladies love romance.' The woman at my table said and sat forward to look directly at me. 'Do you have someone special?'

'No, not like that,' I said. 'I just—'

'Can I ask, what is your job?'

'It's a post in the Chamber of Commerce. Trade development, that sort of thing.'

'But today you sit in a café watching people.' She grinned and nodded. 'You are learning the Berlin way fast.' She called across to a waiter for her bill. 'I must go. Enjoy your stay in our city.'

'Thank you.' I stood up. 'Ah yes, I need to go as well. I want to buy some pictures for my flat.'

'Do you need a painting?' She placed her hand on my arm. 'Come with me. I will take you to a wonderful gallery. Come, it is only across the street.'

We entered the Galleria Brusberg where a young blond woman, in black trousers and shirt wearing a white bow tie, handed us each a flute of Champagne. In the hall was a poster supported on an easel, which simply stated; "Austellung von Marie Heldegard". The polished oak floor reflected images of the paintings hanging around on the white walls. Along the top of one wall, there was a quotation in large black letters. *"The artist is a provocateur. If you want to express yourself, you must present something tangible. Joseph Beuys."*

A group of men in jackets and ties, and some women in cocktail dresses, gestured towards us. The lady with me waved back.

'Look around, you may find something,' she said, and lifted her glass towards the paintings. 'Please, you must excuse me, I am wanted.'

I sauntered around, casually examining the vibrant oil paintings. Most of them were of nude figures wrestling or else in a repose, taking in the sun and bathing by a river.

At the rear of the gallery, a painting depicted a woman in a tussle with a snake coiled around her naked body. I felt a sudden ripple of shock at the closeness of the illuminated central scene framed by a dark background merging away into the shadows. She lay on her back with her hips raised and held the end tip of the snake's tail above her pubic hair. The reptile coiled around her thigh, its body of green, yellow, and black scales in a diamond pattern, wrapped further around her waist. She gripped the neck with her right hand, forcing its fierce head back. Its jaws were wide open, exposing the pin like fangs, and its black, forked tongue flicked towards the right breast.

I shuddered at the sight of the snake's bulging eyes, which stared with a devilish menace. My shirt became damp under my armpits and felt cold. My heart was racing. I wanted to shout something to help, but my mouth was dry. Sipping my drink, I choked on the champagne as if the snake was constricting my throat, tighter and tighter. My breathing became rapid and erratic. My stomach knotted in an irrational panic. I was being emotionally pulled into the painting. The young woman's mouth was partially open, her lips moist, face flushed, hair thrown back, and her eyes half open looked towards me as if beckoning for a kiss. I lifted my hand up to touch her cheek. The scene mesmerized me. Confused, my thoughts switched the context back and forth. Was the snake trying to escape? Was she really in danger of being crushed? Perhaps the serpent was an object of her sexual fantasy?

A shadow slid across the painting, creating an illusion of the black tongue flicking upwards.

'If you like it, buy it,' whispered a warm breath in my ear.

My whole body involuntarily jumped, and I shook, spilling my drink over my shirt and shoes.

'Sorry,' said the woman who had brought me into the gallery.

I stepped back and took a long, hard breath. 'It's my fault. I didn't hear you coming.'

'Well, you must like the painting.' She wiped at my shirt with a napkin. 'You seem fixated.' She pushed the napkin into my empty glass. 'My friends enjoyed watching you.'

I read out the information card, 'Adam and Eve, the Corruption of Man.—Three thousand five hundred euros. Whoa!'

'Too much?' she smiled. 'Why not make an offer?' Then she mumbled. 'Typisch Schotte.'

'It's fantastic. Is there a religious theme?'

'Depends. Are you religious?'

'I don't see Adam.' I pointed to the painting.

'You only see what you believe.' She turned and looked into my eyes. 'What do you think you see?'

'Are you suggesting the snake is Adam?'

She touched the end of my nose with a finger and took hold of my hand. I felt a release of tension as she bumped against me with a friendly familiarity.

'Pity, it's already sold, sorry. Come, Schotte,' she said and linked her arm in mine. 'Let's go to my studio. We will find a painting to fit into your tight wallet.' She walked me towards the door. 'Tschuss,' she called to her friends. The young woman in black took the champagne flute from me before we exited the gallery.

She introduced herself as Marie during the walk along the streets. I became lost in the maze of side lanes and alleyways that she led me along. The most expensive of all her paintings were in the gallery, and art collectors queued to buy them. However, she also had a small version of the Adam and Eve in her studio and thought I would want to buy it.

We turned into a close and then through to a hallway where an old man sat puffing a pipe. He nodded towards Marie and ignore me, but then just shook his head. His aromatic smoke followed our echoing footsteps up the five levels of the dank stairwell.

Marie's studio was bright with the natural light coming through the windows at the side and from the balcony at the back, littered with pots of blue lobelia, lavender, and small evergreen shrubs. A pile of picture frames lay in a corner of the room. Through a half-opened door, I saw a white crumpled duvet on a bed. The smells of paint and a faint familiarity of percolated coffee drifted around the flat.

'Here we are,' Marie said and lifted a picture onto an easel. 'This is exactly what you want.'

I stared, speechless. In the natural light, the illusion of movement from the menacing eyes and forked tongue of the snake gripped my concentration. The girl's expression of sexual ecstasy dominated my thoughts. I wanted this painting.

Marie came up close against me. She touched my nose with her finger, and her warm breath lingered in my ear. 'One thousand,' she whispered, her tongue flicked across my earlobe. 'Euros, cash.' She placed her cheek against mine and held my hand. I kept my attention on the painting. My heart was racing. I had to have it.

'Would you consider six hundred?' I felt a rush of blood flush across my face.

'No!' She let go my hand. 'Typisch Schotte. Nine hundred.'

'Six fifty.' Would she send me away? I breathed in her faint cologne and noticed marks stretch across her shoulder. 'Is that a tattoo?'

Marie stepped back.

'I only have three hundred cash with me.' I had played my last card, perhaps too early.

She removed her blouse and dropped it to the floor. She reached behind and removed her bra. 'Eight hundred,' she said and waited. She puckered a kiss and smiled, brazen and beckoning like the girl in the painting.

The yellow slit of snake eyes on her tattoo stared at me from her shoulder and its tongue caressed her right nipple. The tattoo continued round her back and emerged across her waist.

'Eight hundred.' She undid her skirt and let it fall to the floor. The tail of the snake coiled around her left upper thigh and disappeared beneath her lilac panties.

I looked at the oil painting. I had to buy it.

Grabbing my hand, she pulled me towards the bedroom door and then stopped. She kissed my cheek and said, 'Eight.' She rubbed her fingers over my nose. 'Leave three hundred deposit and tomorrow you can collect the painting.'

Afterwards, Marie had called a taxi to take me home, and I had said goodbye in a happy, euphoric mood without noting her address or telephone number. She hadn't offered the information, nor did I ask.

A waitress approached my table. 'Noch ein Bier?' She had already brought a fresh bottle and a glass.

'Yes, why not?' I passed her the empty one. 'It's still early. Es ist nur halb seben,' Pleased with my German, I grinned.

'You mean thirty minutes past seven,' she said. 'In German, we say the half to the hour. So now... es ist halb acht.'

'Ah! More attention to my German language. Sorry,' I said. 'I've just missed someone.'

'I know,' she laughed, 'Are you Malcolm? Yes?'

'Yes.' I looked up at her. 'Why?'

She placed a business card against the beer bottle and walked away. It was from Marie Hildegrad, showing her address and telephone number.

Falling Stars

The gloomy congregation appeared indifferent as the minister read out the eulogy.

My name is Benjamin Carmichael, and at fifty-two years old, this was my funeral. To me, a surreal moment, as if floating in a euphoric haze as I viewed my coffin draped in the clan tartan shawl and adorned with white lilies. I peeped through the curtains from behind the pulpit, and saw the faces of the crowd. By their demure I sensed an impatient acceptance. Were they saddened by the tale of a tragic loss as imposed on them by the monotonous voice of the minister or merely bored by the ritual? Surely, they had been expecting this day and eventually their long suffering would be over. Soon, the cremation will turn the coffin into ash and the body's soul will flutter free in a plume of white smoke. Afterwards, they will continue with their lives, relieved of guilty retributions.

I pulled up my coat collar against the chill of the draught coming up through the floorboards, where I hid behind the black drapes. To quell my urge to laugh, I stifled a coughed.

My decline began three years ago, when for a while I just didn't seem my usual vibrant self. Horrified, I knew something was wrong when I received the news confirming my journey towards a premature death. The doctor had asked me to lie on my side and pull my legs up into the foetal position. Her smile and the laughter lines around her eyes made me uneasy as she spread my bare buttocks. Perhaps, and I might have appreciated the experience and procedure more, and maybe—just maybe—if she had warmed the gel before she put her icy, gloved finger up my anus.

'Oh, dear.' She frowned. 'It feels like an enlarged walnut. We'll conduct further examinations and blood tests. To be certain.'

Walnut! I would have expected her to use medical terminology, but it seems any reference to testicles, or the prostate gland, is analogous with nuts.

'The nurse will take your blood,' she said, and gave me a smile of defeated reassurance.

Her words made me laugh. I had the sudden vision in my mind of a female vampire in a skimpy nurse's uniform, embedding her fangs deep into my carotid artery as she drained the life from me. A hopeful, illogical reaction to the doctor's news.

After three years of failing treatments, they admitted me into the cancer research centre. That's what private health insurance gets you, your own room, and the privilege of being a guinea pig to medical science. It delighted me that all the students could embellish their knowledge as they took turns to probe my swelling tumour in my anus. The balding consultant lectured on about my degenerative condition, now slowly creeping throughout my body. Apparently, I had left it too late for a radical prostatectomy.

I would smile at his cheerful mantra laced with an air of defeatism. "Good morning, Mr Carmichael. You're still with us today." As if a miracle in the night had organised my escape, perhaps to a better place. Certainly, I could think no place worse than this clinic where I was methodically dying under the scrutiny of medical experimentation.

Oh, the family and friends came visiting, always tearful and full of hopeless encouragement, but as time passed, they appeared less frequently, and with less tears. I had become a physiological burden and a nuisance throughout their daily routine. It was the knowing and not knowing with the contradictions of fate and hope that pained them. I gently encouraged a view of acceptance that would distance their grief from all intrusive thoughts and to continue with their lives as I slowly degenerated towards bodily disintegration.

I did not mind the prospect of dying, however the slow pace of the journey and the constant bobbing between episodes of pain and euphoric highs of morphine induced hallucinations became unbearable. A frustration similar to waiting for a delayed long-haul flight.

I once played profession football until my knees protested, so afterwards I formed a business selling sports luggage. During a trade exhibition, I met Carol. We agreed a partnership to expand my range with handbags and sold them through her fashion shops. The arrangement succeeded and over a year, our personal relationship also blossomed. We married soon afterwards, and life proved generous to us, blessing us with two children, Mike and Vanessa.

One late evening, I sat despondent by the window in the clinic, tearfully fearful of my fate. It proved a difficult day following radiation and a dose of bisphosphonates. I observed the spectacle of stars in the clear night sky. Occasionally, bright flares of meteorites streaked towards Earth before they burned out in the atmosphere. Rosanne, a hospital cleaner, came to me and wiped my face with a sweet-smelling tissue.

'You only die if you want to,' she said, and stood beside me.

'What choice do I have?'

'Falling stars, they are the souls of angels returning to Earth.'

'What!' Indignant about my outburst, I moderated my tone. 'Yes, of course, angels.'

'Try this.' She took a small flask from her apron pocket. 'Drink some berry tea.'

I sipped at the acrid juice as she placed her hand on my head. She closed her eyes and recited a prayer. Once finished with her religious ritual, she hugged me.

'Dying is natural. Make a choice and let it go,' she said.

Next morning, I sat up encouraged and cheered by Rosanne's rigid belief in the power of faith and sweet tea. I hobbled across to the window. How I missed being outdoors in the fresh air. Occasionally, I marvelled at the sight of rain and the drops running down the glass like the tears on my face. Then I noticed them. I watched my wife Carol get out of a white Range Rover in the car park. Douglas, my business partner, hugged and kissed her more lovingly than any mutual friendship should dictate. They began laughing beyond grief. At this, my cancer inflamed and raged through my bones, and my heart thumped as it pumped its fiery liquid through my veins.

She came up to my room alone and sat next to the bed. She held my hand loosely, avoiding the permanently attached intravenous needle.

'You're looking better today,' she said, her face blank and drained of emotional expression.

'I know.'

'It's a lovely sunny day outside.' She hid her disdain in the stare of her hazel eyes.

'How are Mike and Vanessa?'

'You mustn't worry about us.' She lifted her iPhone. 'Look, our time in St Lucia.'

As she flicked through the pictures of her and Vanessa, I noticed Douglas lingering in the background, but I said nothing. I had no strength to argue and was unwilling to change the mood. Why should I judge? I didn't recall seeing Mike in any of these recent images.

From my vantage point concealed in the church, I had tried to judge their expressions. It seemed so obvious now. Carol kept looking back down the aisle as if waiting for someone to fill the empty seat beside her. She clung on to Vanessa's hand. I couldn't detect their emotions or see tears on their faces, looking tanned by the healthy exposure to nature and fresh air. Where was Mike? Filling the remaining seats sat more relatives and business acquaintances, all dressed in black, looking like vultures ready to pick and clean the bones of some leftover carcass.

Back in the hospital research ward, I had indulged Rosanne's constant attention with her insistence of prayer as I listened and sipped sweet berry tea. How could she have so much belief when my family and the doctors had all given up? Her reliance on the power of God replaced the limitations of medical treatments. She trusted in the words of the Bible and palmetto berries. She believed in fate and had made provisions for her passing. I learned she was not the employed cleaner after all, but enjoyed working on the ward, as it helped her spend what remained of her life being useful. She also introduced me to her friends and family, a group of people who had formed a deep belief in the regeneration of angels. They reminded me of hippies from the sixties with a naïve idealism of a perfect world, who accepted the failings of human bodies and believed that medical science would never surpass the inevitable end of old age. They preached self-determination and the right to make choices They offered me an end-of-life plan, one that I found exciting and so comforting.

From my late twenties, I had built up a leather handbag and suitcase business worth millions. Douglas, in my absence, had taken over the concern in complete disregard to my son, Mike, who held a minor managerial position. Ever since my confinement, Mike had formed an unhealthy distaste for Douglas and became determined to surpass him to continue the family name.

My house was mortgage free, like the holiday home in St. Lucia. Carol and Vanessa had financial security, and I accepted Douglas might be part of their lives. Still, I couldn't help my notion of failure and, although it may seem illogical, I blamed him for my cancer. Mike reluctantly sold my share in the business to pay for my trip of a lifetime, my choice, and my end-of-life plan. For my life to fade away in a stuffy hospital bed should not be an experience that anyone wanted.

As I looked around the congregation, I mentally said goodbye. I had made the right choice. I sneaked out the back of the church and met Mike waiting in his car. We sped along the motorway towards the aerodrome and to the lift-off point for my final destination. I asked Mike how he had arranged a body in the coffin. Ah, don't worry, he told me, earthly matters should no longer be my concern. Besides, he will soon have full control of the business in a few weeks.

Rosanne's hand warmed mine as we sat on the escalator chair, taking us into the spacecraft. A sense of relief and an awareness of self-control washed over me as I embarked on this last and final stage of our journey. Rosanne had a radiant expression and smiled. Behind, as well as in front of us, lines of other chairs took people into the same rocket. Although the sense of excitement was subdued, every face glowed with warmth and accepted happiness. They split us into two groups, the inward and the outward bound.

The inward-bound group, all of whom had a terminal illness, would fall from space and burn up in the Earth's atmosphere. They would become the falling angels, as Rosanne believed. The outward-bound group, containing the older adults of healthy people, would drift in small capsules away into the void, where the occupants could marvel at the enormity of the universe as their life slowly passed away. Their bodies frozen in time, and perhaps collide with a distant place, where it may be possible from their DNA to create a colony of human life.

In orbit, we looked down at the glowing planet suspended by the gravitation hold from the sun. Its rays warmed us through the viewing portals. From the spacecraft, I observed for my first and last time the blue planet, and my emotions erupted in jubilant happiness. Rosanne squeezed my arm; a saviour through my darkest moments in the clinic and for me a beautiful angel. My time came to descend to the planet where I was born and where I had the humble privilege of a wonderful existence.

Maria

Carl Mackenzie glimpsed a woman passing nearby in the crowd, and his heartbeat raced. He stumbled into a pushcart and sat on its edge. He needed a moment. Was it Maria? After a few deep breaths, he drank some water and regained his balance. Should he speak to her? What would he say after all these years? Possibly she might speak first. Using a wet handkerchief, he wiped his brow and neck to cool himself. Sweat crept under his armpits. The heat of the Mediterranean made him feel lightheaded, and his shallow breathing sucked in the warm air. He wandered on, searching among the bustling groups. After this glance at her head and shoulders, he could be wrong, since he did not see her face.

The letter was an enigmatic invitation, and although dubious, he arranged a flight to Naples and travelled by train to the fishing port.

Auctioneers shouted their prices for fish, and the buyers dragged boxes away, scraping them over the wet concrete. In front of him, labourers grunted as they hauled a yellowfin tuna along the aisle. They shouted obscenities, and he jumped out of their way before being pushed. The throng gave him a headache and the ripe smell cloyed over his clothes and hair. Nausea ascended from his stomach. He dashed and pushed past some burly men who protested by blowing cigarette smoke into his face.

On the dockside, he sat on a mooring post and lifted his head towards the breeze drifting across the harbour. The squawking of seagulls squabbling over floating fish offal was an accompanying chorus to his thoughts. Did he see Maria? Perhaps he saw an apparition conjured up from suppressed memories that haunted him for years, provoking feelings of guilt and shame. He treasured those memories of her warm smiles and recurring dreams of reuniting their love. But also, he suffered from cold sweats and nightmares from which he awoke emotionally fragile and depressed. An inexplicable message in this recent letter intrigued him, and his curiosity motivated his return to Italy.

Twenty years ago, he disembarked onto this dockside with pack mules carrying radio equipment on their backs. His task was to set up a divisional re-broadcasting station in the hills above Sessa Aurunca with a radio line of sight over the valley towards the river Garigliano. The geographical feature designated by the Germans as the Gustav Line.

Carl stretched his left leg to release its numbness. A few consulting surgeons, over the years, considered amputation after a series of infections and recurring ulcerations. However, the stab wounds eventually healed. He ambled back towards the guest house, where he would change. He waited on the pavement as a blue car went past, driven by the woman he saw in the market, and she turned right towards Aurunca.

In his hotel room, he stripped off and let the chill from the air conditioning sweep over his body. In the shower, as water washed down his back, his thoughts drifted. He had only arrived, and yet, was it possible he saw Maria in the fish market? What was he doing coming back to Italy? He washed and rubbed off the soap trapped in the long scar on his leg. Was he prepared for the worst?

Through the coach window, Carl looked across the Italian countryside with its fields of tomato plants and irrigation channels. In the distance, workers were tending to the vines on the hillsides. Cypress trees lined on each side of the road, giving him an impression of a civilisation structured in uniformity and orderliness. He leaned back and enjoyed the vista as the cool air from the blower drifted over his face.

Years ago, wild vegetation grew over this area, and the journey on foot was precarious with frequent air attacks. He had stumbled around bomb craters, and from destroyed vehicles frequent minor explosions startled the pack mules.

In Sessa Aurunca, he got off the bus. He had the nostalgic idea of retracing his route up the mountain to where, so long ago, he set up the radio station.

The track through the vineyards was a gentle climb, and the sweat dripped from his chin. Why did he leave the comfort of the bus? He stopped and stared back towards the town's cathedral, noting the wall where a retreating German unit executed a group of partisans.

He followed a stream and after an hour of a stumbling, in a zig-zag scramble through the scrub, he found a track along the ridge. Further on, he reached an area of large granite rocks and climbed onto one.

From this place, he had watched the smoke rise along the Garigliano riverbank as a battle raged.

Today, the view towards the river was tranquil, and he traced the mountain road down towards Torelle.

He took out the letter and read once more there was important news that Maria had longed to tell him. If he came to visit, he would learn the details. There was no signature, and he did not recognise the writing. In Maria's letter to him, eighteen years ago, she had begged him to come back to Italy. She did not answer his reply, instead her father wrote and promised to kill him.

The path led to the road and to the old rendezvous point where the company quartermaster once delivered resupplies to the troop. A cairn now stood at this spot, and he read the name on the plaque.

Georgio Donatello Pastore
Ventiquattro Anni
Eroe

He slumped onto his knees. Shaking, he drained the last mouthful of water from his bottle. It was a memorial for the man who tried to kill him, the man he shot in self-defence. His eyes welled up. Who was to blame? He blamed Hitler; he blamed the world for the madness of the war, but still he knew this death had nothing to do with the battle for Monte-Cassino. It was about the intensity of love, family honour and a stupid waste of a life.

That night, his meeting with Maria in the barn above the village was a passionate affair with promises of an eternal future of hope and happiness. He accepted the fresh bread, chicken, and eggs she gave him for the troop and departed along the rough track up the mountain. Someone was following, so he hid and waited. Georgio appeared and was in a confrontational mood. He accused Carl of dishonour to his family, and of raping his sister. Suddenly, he pulled out a switchblade and struck out at Carl, slashing his thigh. To avoid the knife and a second lunge, he rolled away over the ground. When Georgio rushed at him, he pulled out his pistol and fired several shots. Infuriated, he kicked at the man's dead body.

Maria warned him how her father would never accept them being married, but she didn't care, and she intended to leave Torelle and settle with him in Scotland. Nothing would keep them apart, but it seemed Georgio had intended to preserve the family's honour.

The ghost of Georgio re-emerged in his mind, and he rubbed his fingers along the letters on the plaque as if seeking forgiveness. He got up, stretched the numbness in his legs, and carried on along the path, taking his time downhill towards the village. Physically, it was easy, but he struggled to form an explanation. What was he going to discuss with Maria?

That night, the noise of his shots alerted the troop guard who came running. The medic bandaged his leg, then took him to a military field hospital for treatment. He never knew what happened to the body of Georgio and never asked. Perhaps this was the information alluded to in the letter. Did someone know the truth? After all, he had lied to the Military Police during their rudimentary investigation, and they accepted his version about challenging the man for spying on their location. The incident was closed.

The instructions in the letter were specific, go to Salvatore's, order an expresso from the server in English and just wait.

He reached the barn on the slope above the village, a place where his love for Maria kindled and raged through his dreams ever since. The charcoaled remains of the roof lay amongst the ruined walls where a thick patch of nettles and ivy grew. A surge of tiredness drained through him. Was the decision of returning to Torelle futile? Who would meet him in the Salvatore café?

He walked on along the boundary wall to the cemetery where he noticed a recently placed display of cut flowers. He strolled toward the graves. It was a moment of procrastination as the sight of the dilapidated barn lessened his enthusiasm for the meeting in the café.

The name carved on a marble headstone confirmed his presumption; Donatello Umberto Pastore, Maria's father. Unashamedly, he smiled as a release of tension wash through him. He looked around and noted a newly polished stone further back in the family plot, and he read the name on the headstone. A jolt struck his heart, and his left leg trembled with muscle spasm.

Maria Cristina Francesca Pastore
Figlia amata
1924 – 45

Carl checked the timings at the bus stop. it was another hour before the next service departed back to the fishing port. He wandered into the plaza, avoiding Salvatore's café on the east side. Customers occupied the outdoor tables, enjoying the warmth of the afternoon sun. Instead, he made his way along the opposite side of the square to an open-air restaurant and took a seat facing the road.

He ordered a starter of tomato salad, a main dish of spaghetti carbonara and a jug of water, then he leaned back to observe the activity across the square and particularly Salvatore's. Although the letter did not mention a specific time, it suggested he should arrive this week, and on any afternoon at his convenience. His first instinct was to ignore the proposal, but the idea of seeing Maria overpowered his reluctance. What did he have to lose? What now? From the revelation of Maria's grave, there was no reason to stay. Was this a trap for revenge?

A Fiat car stopped at Salvatore's. At the same moment, the server brought his salad and bread with a dish of olive oil. Distracted, he didn't notice anyone enter the café from the car.

After he finished his carbonara, the same blue Fiat drove into a carpark space facing the restaurant.

"Signor MacKenzie, Si." A server approached his table.

"Yes, I—"

"Un bicchiere gratuito di vino bianco," he interrupted and placed the glass of wine next to the water jug. He waved a table napkin in the air as he sauntered back to the bar.

Carl sipped the wine. He put the glass down slowly. Someone knew he was here.

A car door slammed. He looked up. A young woman came striding across the carpark. Maria! Impossible. She skipped off the pavement, crossed the road, and marched onto the restaurant patio. She pulled out a chair at his table and sat. The hair, the dark eyes, the sultry confidence, Carl felt a surge of adrenalin bolt through him, a ghost, an illusion. She was the woman he saw earlier in the fish market. A young woman about eighteen or nineteen years old, not Maria.

"Signor Carl Mackenzie," she said.

He stared at her face, the same face that smiled at him in his dreams, in the moonlight, in the barn.

"Signor Carl Mackenzie." She reached out and touched his hand.

"Yes."

"Mi chiamo Silvia, tua figlia."

"Silvia was my mother's name," he said.

"Yes, I am Silvia Maria Cristina Pastore." She gripped his hand tightly. "Mia madre è morta quando sono nato." Her eyes welled up and watered. "My mother died as I was born."

Ma Blake's Bar

'Let's go.' Allan sprinted towards the swamp. He ran through the coarse grass and screamed as he leapt over the boundary ditch. Landing short of the edge, he sank up to his knees. Desperate, he grasped hold of a tree root to drag himself out against the suction of the mud. His left shoe was stuck fast, and his foot slipped free. A murky effluent oozed to fill the holes, and air bubbles gurgled from the slime as if his lost sneaker were whimpering for help.

'Well,' he shouted to his friends standing on the road. 'Come on then, you twats.'

Allan sat down and laughed. Perhaps this fall was an ominous warning of how each decision he made from now on would be precarious. So! He wasn't superstitious. Not like Mai Ling, who would chide him with; "disaster follow disaster", but she was not here. What would she be doing? It was her smile that entrapped him, pulling him into her world of oriental wisdom and warmth between her silken sheets. Four months ago, he said goodbye, four months since he breathed the fresh jasmine in her hair as she sat astride him. She had held him tight and kept repeating how he must write every day. Ridiculous, it seems now.

'Bugger,' he shouted. 'Are you twats coming or not?'

He took off his remaining Adidas trainer and stood up. Holding the laces, he swung it around a few times, then let it go to fly over a clump of bull reeds. Momentarily, he heard a splash. A grey crane appeared from behind the rushes and silently glided above his head. The bird floated effortlessly through the air with the elegance so like Mai Ling during her morning ritual of Tai Chi. It flapped its wide wings to gain height above the mango bushes, and he watched as it travelled towards the sea.

In his socks, he hobbled and tiptoed along the dirt path, avoiding the exposed roots and the broken shells from dead land crabs. His chinos stank of putrid, decaying vegetation. He had laundered them that morning, now seemingly a waste of time and a reminder of all things pointless.

Yesterday, he discovered this shortcut to Ma Blake's bar, a haven of pirated rum. An isolated stilted shack of weathered wood with a rusted tin roof covered in a splattering of guano from passing frigate birds.

After a few steps, he turned and looked back. 'Come on dickheads,' he shouted and waved a V sign.

'Hang on,' bellowed Caz as he helped Nick drag an abandoned pallet from the roadside. They swung it back and forth twice to gain momentum before dropping it into the ditch.

'This place stinks to hell,' mumbled Caz and he wiped his hands on the back of Nick's T-shirt, who turned and punched him on his shoulder.

One at a time, they leapt over the mire, using the pallet as a step, and ran to catch up with Allan.

'What a shit hole,' said Caz, and he grabbed hold of Allan's arm. 'Are you sure she'll be there?'

Allan shrugged him off. 'I couldn't care less,' he said. 'There'll be rum.' He tugged at his earlobe as his internal voice mimicked; "no, no, you not-drink", a chastisement from Mai Ling. She was as delicate as the lotus, and born in the Year of the Dragon; smooth as porcelain. What is she doing now?

A pair of mongrel bitches, their teats flapping, came barking to stand guard at the top of the slope. They wrinkled their snouts, showing large, yellowed teeth as they growled and barked.

'Hell!' Caz dashed back a few paces.

'Easy, easy,' shouted a young woman from an upstairs window. 'Down Sissy...down...in the den.'

The dogs wagged their tails and sniffed at Allan's trousers a few times before they retreated out of the late afternoon glare. The dogs slouched down under the shade of the shack, and a group of pups crawled over them, seeking sustenance.

Caz gave Allan a nudge. 'Is that her?' he whispered, staring at her.

'Yep.'

'Come you den,' she called and leaned out of the window. 'You want food.' Her perk breasts pushed against her dress and her nipples showed through the faded cotton.

Caz stared.

'Go inside,' she said and ducked back into the room.

'It's this way.' Allan pointed to a side door.

Caz slapped Nick's bottom. 'Who calls dogs Sissy?' he said. 'Stupid name for dogs.'

The darkness inside the bar blinded them, and they jostled each other by the doorway. For a moment they remained still, letting their eyes become accustomed to the dimness before feeling their way along the wall and stumbling into the furniture. They found the chairs and sat down. A soft shuffling sound came towards them. Someone thumped a plastic bowl of ice onto the table. They jerked back in their seats and stared up at the silhouette of a rotund woman.

She shouted, 'Hey Jez man, open de shutter. Dem boys here as blind as ma arse.' She gave a screeching laugh.

A shutter opened at the end of the room, and in the daylight, they saw Ma Blake. Her skin gleamed like polished ebony on her Caucasian features and her wide grin rumpled the crow's feet around her eyes. Using her hand, she wiped some moisture from her face and then dried it through her head of short, curly hair.

'Rice, beans an' chicken or cow foot soup, an' cola, you wan cola?' She looked at each of them.

'Rum and coke,' said Allan. 'I'm not hungry.'

'Man, there's a swampy smell by you.' She cocked her head towards him.

'Just Belikin for us.' Caz pointed at Nick.

'No Belikin!'

'Okay, just rum with cola.' Caz shrugged.

Music burst out loud across the room.

'Hey, Jez man,' Ma shouted and moved off towards the bar. She turned down the volume just as the chorus started.

'You'd think they'd have beer,' said Caz. 'We should've gone down the Belle Vue.' He tapped Nick on the shoulder, and he nodded.

Ma Blake brought them the cola and wiped the dust off the bottle tops with her pinny. She pulled the cork from an encrusted bottle of rum.

'Now you boys drink slow.' She glared at them. 'Listen, good now.' She waited for a response.

Caz and Nick nodded.

'I have emptied the washer, cause there're some clothes need a washing.' She poked Allan in the arm. 'You should no come through de swamp, dem fever is bad.' She poked him again and then headed past the bar to the kitchen.

Allan picked up the bottle and felt the rough barnacles bite into his hand as he poured the dark liquid into the glasses. "No, no, you must not drink," Mai Ling pleaded in his mind. He added some cola and reached towards the plastic bowl, and changed his mind. Once before, he had discovered beetles and pieces of weeds frozen amongst the crushed ice. He took a large gulp and burst into a gasping fit.

'Hell, this is the dog's bollocks.'

The eighty-degree proof scorched his oesophagus and sent a warm flush around his stomach. An immediate rush of blood eased the tightness of his muscles, and he relaxed back into his chair. "You no get so happy"; ah, Mai Ling, who do I love?

The first mouthful was always the best; it evaporated his guilt, drowned his anxiety, fed his cravings, and justified his addiction to the pirate's curse. Who cared if it contained fifty known poisons and others that science had yet to identify? Ma Blake's One-Barrel-Rum was an elixir that made him feel alive, amorous, and invincible. "You no go mad… please," Mai Ling was fading. The taste of rum with its anaesthetic effect cushioned his thoughts, yet he so much wanted to be in her arms and stroke her face. What would she be doing now? Did his little lover sleep alone at night?

'I can't drink this crap.' Caz emptied his rum into the plastic bowl. He poured some cola into his glass and stood the bottle in amongst the ice.

The young woman from the upstairs window strolled into the bar. Caz stared, watching her every move. She wore a short tight skirt and an armless glittering top above a bare midriff. Stroking the hair hanging over her left shoulder, she smiled at Jez, who turned the reggae music up. Oscillating her arms, she performed a dance across the floor, swaying her hips above her bare thighs.

Nick looked away and grabbed for his drink.

'Hola! Allan,' she said and stood behind him, massaging his shoulders. 'Ma says I should get your pants off.' She kissed the back of his head.

He reached up and took hold of her hand. 'You'd love that.'

'Hey Carmen,' Ma shouted. 'Stop fooling and bring him out here.' She waved some clothes in the air.

Caz sat forward and smiled to get attention. Nick thumped him on his leg under the table.

Carmen pulled Allan by his hand and led him towards the kitchen. Mai Ling pleaded, "no big ideas."

From behind the bar, Ma threw him a pair of cotton shorts and a shirt. 'You should not take the swamp path. It smells bad.'

In the washroom, Carmen loaded powder into the machine and turned to watch him undress. She came over and helped him off with his T-shirt; she rubbed his shoulders and slipped her hand down over his biceps.

'You want to come upstairs?' She stroked along his body and down towards his buttocks.

'Carmen, I…' he mumbled.

Their noses touched, and her close musky aura engulfed him; a release of testosterone pulsated around his groin and his breathing became irregular and rapid. She brushed her cheek over his.

'I do special for you,' she whispered and flicked his ear with her tongue. 'Only fifty-five dollars.'

His urge for warm female comfort rushed up his body, but Mai Ling raged, "no getting so hot." He eased Carmen's hands off and stood back from her.

'Oh Carmen.' he said. 'You know I can't.' He grabbed the clothes and pulled on the shorts and shirt.

Carmen smiled. 'You always need more rum… first.' She laughed and gathered up his clothes and threw them into the washer.

'Dem flip-flops over there are for you.' She pointed.

Back in the bar, Caz and Nick had gone. Allan poured and drunk two glasses of rum in quick succession.

Ma came across with a mosquito coil and tried to light it. 'Dem boys no good. What dem said about Carmen?' She shook her lighter. 'Dem gone, cause dem wan beer.' She tried clicking the lighter again. 'Jez, he gives dem a run to town.'

He took a large swig of rum, coughed, and spluttered, sending some of it across the table. Ma's lighter sparked and ignited the alcoholic fumes. She dashed her cloth over the blue flames and wiped the table.

'You should not drink so much,' she said and lit the coil. 'Captain Blake's is no good for you.' She picked up the bottle and took it back to the bar.

Everyone boasted about the dangers of the rum. Who cares if you sip it slow it soothes the mind. He leaned back and let it swill around in his mouth. Even the ugly pirate in the painting on the wall knew about addiction to this fermented liquid. He smiled back at the fixating eyes of the buccaneer and silently toasted him for plundering the Royal Fortune a century ago and pirating its cargo of One Barrel. Carmen's great, great relation of sorts, she had said, and they hanged him in London for his Caribbean swashbuckling.

The daylight dimmed, and Carmen swayed around, lighting the oil lamps on the bar. He watched as she closed the shutters and then changed the music to a hypnotic beat of steel drums. She picked up a bottle along with a plate of cut limes and swayed across the room. She sat next to him.

'Here,' she said, 'Ma says no more rum.' She poured some tequila into a glass, drunk it up in one, and sucked on a lime wedge. 'You wanna to try some.' She undid her ponytail and shook her hair.

Allan felt the heat of the tequila rush down to his stomach and mix with the rum. He grabbed up a lime and sucked at the acerbic juice to lessen the harsh taste of the liquor. Smoke from the coil spiralled around them and his heart synchronised with the rhythmic music. He closed his eyes. The image of the crane gliding over the trees floated in his mind, disappearing far out over the sea, searching for Mai Ling.

Carmen rubbed her hand over his thigh, higher at each stroke and under his shorts. He clasped her wrist and lifted it up to his face. Her skin was soft and warm as he caressed it over his cheek.

She smiled and leaned in close. 'Are you feeling warm?' She snuggled her nose against his ear. He breathed in the scent of jasmine from her hair.

In the deep mango forest of Belize,
Amongst the ancient mighty Mayan ruin,
In a temptress trap full of love's disease,
With tequila's heat and full voodoo moon.
Carmens's beauty masks the mosquito's bite.

Don't tell Vanessa

Brian stared at the litter between the rail tracks. He balanced on the edge of the platform and rocked back and forth on the balls of his feet. He waited. Soon, someone will clean him up into a black plastic bag along with the cigarette butts and crushed cola tins. Perhaps the label will read, "Brian, human waste and other rubbish".

There was a sense of crackling inside the back of his head as the Prozac melted the crystallised ends of his synapses. What could he do to fill the numbed emptiness in his mind? Nothing. An internal voice confirmed he was a zombie these days, and without a meaningful purpose, it was time to say goodbye.

Something hit him on the back of his legs. He turned and picked up the little handbag with a small teddy tied to its buckle. A small girl stopped skipping and stared at him. He stepped back from the platform edge and handed it to the child.

'Thank you,' she said. 'Teddy doesn't like trains.'

Her mother grabbed the girl's free hand just as the Intercity roared past. She dragged the girl away, who looked back at Brian and giggled. The slipstream blew and ruffled her loose hair and flapped it around her head and face. A sparkle of happiness in the girl's eyes registered somewhere in the void of Brian's thoughts. He tried to smile.

The local train arrived moments later. He boarded his usual carriage and travelled to work, where he was going to be sacked.

'I don't support their decision, but you are lucky,' Anderson told him. 'HR has agreed to keep you but move you out of Bristol to Leeds.' Anderson leaned forward on her desk. 'You've still got your job. It's a warning. Find your inspiration in Tetley tea instead of Glenmorangie.'

Brian strode into the office and shook Mike's hand with exaggerated firmness.

'Welcome back!' Mike said. 'Hark at you. A new suit and an ironed shirt.'

'It's fantastic to be back in Bristol,' he said, and adjusted the Windsor knot of his tie. 'You're looking fit. Still playing golf then?'

'I do my best,' Mike said. 'How long has it been since you left?' He sat down with a bounce on his leather chair.

'Three years,' Brian pointed to the empty desk in the corner. 'Will that be mine?'

'No, no. The software section is upstairs.' Mike handed him a sticky-note with his home telephone number. 'Agnes wants you to come round on Sunday and bring Susan. She's desperate for gossip. How is Susan?'

'Yes, Susan.' Brian walked over to the window and looked down into the street.

'She is okay. Is she?' Mike said.

'Susan's fine.' Brian's eyes fixated on the carpet. 'I've an initial interview with bossy Anderson, and need to go. I'll call you.' He slumped his shoulders and hurried towards the door.

'Wait!' Mike called. 'You don't know! Jackie Anderson is missing.'

Mike heard the garden gate squeak and looked over the top of his Sunday Mail and saw Brian. He wore light fawn trousers and a woollen chequered pullover.

'Anyone home?' Brian called.

Toby, the Labrador, barked and ran up from the bottom of the garden, alerting Agnes, who was on her knees, pulling chickweed from amongst the dahlias.

'Brian, I'm glad you came,' Mike said.

Agnes rushed into the gazebo on the patio and dropped her garden gloves onto a chair.

'Brian, you are looking well.' She stretched forward and hugged him. 'Ah! New aftershave,' she said. 'Please, sit down. Is Susan not with you?'

'Oh yes, Susan,' he said, and then sat down.

Mike and Agnes looked at each other. Toby pushed forward and put his head onto Brian's lap.

'We're divorced.'

'When!' Agnes shouted.

'Not long after we moved to Leeds,' Brian stroked Toby's head.

'I'm sorry, Oh dear.' Agnes gave a brief moan and sat down on top of her garden gloves. 'So that's why you didn't keep in touch. Do you need a drink?'

'No, No. Well, a tea would be nice.' He fidgeted with the dog's ears. 'I'm married to Vanessa now and–
–'

'Vanessa,' Agnes said, 'Where is she?'

'She's in the car waiting until I—'

'Bring her in,' Agnes ordered. 'You left her sitting in the car. Unbelievable!'

Brian introduced Vanessa, who wore a pleated sports skirt, a matching pullover to his, and her blond hair tied in a ponytail. She sat down and hit Toby as she crossed her legs, knocking off one of her tartan plimsolls.

'Oops, sorry,' she said and slipped her shoe back on. She took off her soft leather gloves. 'O dear, I should've left these with my golf bag.'

Over tea, Brian explained. In Leeds, Susan left with the boys to stay with her mother in York. After the divorce, she married an old school friend almost immediately.

Mike knew Brian was omitting the actual issue that broke up the marriage, one that almost cost him his job. However, he saw the subtle physical changes in him. He had a light tan, and the loose midriff flab had gone.

Smiling at Vanessa as the pastry from Agnes's strawberry tart crumbled around his lips, Brian explained how they met two years ago at the swimming pool. A doctor had advised him to exercise or else start a funeral expense policy. What else could he do? So, he hired Vanessa as his personal trainer to rejuvenate his sporting interests.

Toby walked around the patio, wagged his tail, and gave the occasional light bark.

'Vanessa, would you like to come along?' Agnes picked up the dog's lead. 'It's time for Toby's walk.'

After the women left, they discussed how Jackie Anderson's proposal to outsource the software section was on hold. The shock of her being found dead meant the entire project stalled. Brian appreciated, she had accepted him back and sorry to learn of her tragic demise. However, he was worried as the position in Leeds was no longer an option, and his proposal to keep the work 'in house', and take over Anderson's post, worried him. Besides, Vanessa was looking forward to settling in Bristol and she wanted to start a family.

'Are you not too old, you know?' Mike smirked. 'Thinking about a new family?'

'Thanks,' Brian said. 'Yes, at forty-five, you're right. But then again, Vanessa's in her early thirties. You know, that brooding age.'

'Brian, remind me. Didn't you have a vasectomy? I remember Susan made you—'

'Whatever you do, Mike. Don't tell Vanessa.'

Agnes and Vanessa stood on top of the escarpment looking towards the Clifton suspension bridge, over the Avon gorge. They watched the seagulls float in the air as Vanessa spoke to Agnes about her plans for a family. Since she aborted in her teens, she thought this might be the reason nothing was happening and was the problem. Shocked at what she was saying by opening up about her personal issues. She asked Agnes not to mention this to anyone, especially not to Brian.

However, Agnes seemed preoccupied and pointed to the woods on the distant hill.

'It was a few miles beyond those woods where they found Jackie. Last week, fly-tipped like an old sofa. Why do men do such awful things?'

Vanessa was silent as they walked along the path and wondered if she could trust Agnes. They sat on a wooden bench under a sycamore tree and Agnes released Toby from his lead; off he ran, racing past the grass cutter and across the field towards another dog. Agnes shouted and chased after him, leaving Vanessa alone amongst the whirling samara fluttering from the branches. The image of the poor murdered woman and why men do such awful things made Vanessa shudder and the smell of the cut grass provoked a shameful memory. She reached into her pocket for a tissue and decided never to tell Agnes.

Dad had mowed the lawn before taking Mum and her brother, Ben, to his school football. They wanted her to come along, but she had pulled the sun bed out of the shed and relished the opportunity for some peace to read in the garden.

She didn't realise how long Uncle Derek had been standing there, staring down at her. He asked to borrow the garden shears from the shed. When she looked around in the shed, he grabbed her. She struggled, but he forced her face down amongst the compost on the potting table. He muffled her protesting cries and sobs with the oily rag used to wipe the mower and then he slid her bikini bottoms aside to ram her from behind, again and again. When he turned to leave, Vanessa grabbed the garden fork and stabbed at his legs but missed.

He laughed and warned not to tell. It was her own fault. So, grow up.

Mum and Dad arrived home late with Ben and his leg in a plaster cast because of a fracture sustained from a hard tackle. Vanessa tried to talk to her mother, but she was going on about who was to blame for Ben's accident. She then screamed at Vanessa for using all the hot water by showering in the afternoon, of all times. Dad nagged on and on about the mess in the shed and having left its door wide open. Why don't they listen? Perhaps it was her fault. Her indignation poured into a tear sodden pillow behind her slammed bedroom door.

Back at boarding school, Vanessa showed the pregnancy result to Christina, the only person she could trust. Christina came from a farm in Cumbria and often experienced lambing with its messy slime. They hid in the attic with a bottle of methylated spirit and a flask of boiled water. Christina fiddled with a folded coat hanger until she dragged the embryo out. Amazed at the tiny nodule, they placed it into a matchbox and buried it in the woods with tears and prayers, asking for forgiveness.

The infection required antibiotics from the doctor, who warned that such foolishness might affect her future ability to have children.

'Vanessa, you are crying.' Agnes returned with Toby in his lead.

'No, it's just an allergy, from the grass cutting.' Vanessa wiped her face with a paper tissue.

'Come on. Let's get back. I have some antihistamine at home.'

Agnes waved to Brian and Vanessa as they drove off.

'It's a shame they can't have children.' Agnes said to Mike as she closed the garden gate.

'I don't think Brian told her about the vasectomy.'

'Vasectomy, oh dear. She never mentioned that.' Agnes grabbed Mike's arm. "Unbelievable!'

'Agnes, it's none of our business. Don't get involved.'

Vanessa argued how adoption required background checks and would reveal Brian as being unsuitable because of his mental history. The adopted children would never be real siblings and yes, she wanted at least two.

Brian bought the Sunday Times not just to read about the arrest of Jackie Anderson's murderer. A neighbour who had been stalking her had reacted with violence when rejected. He was more interested in the magazine article on adoption and the picture of a photogenic baby looking for a home.

'The clinic results show I am normal,' Vanessa said and puffed up her soft pillow on the bed and sat back. 'I think you need to go for a check-up.'

'Look at that rain.' Brian pointed to the window and passed a glass of orange juice to Vanessa. 'If it doesn't ease, I think we can forget about golf.'

'I've booked you in with Doctor Chambers for Wednesday,' she said, ignoring his attempt at distraction. 'Please, make sure you take time off work.'

Brian squirmed around in bed. Why did the women in his life want control of his 'Vas Deferens'? Susan insisted on the operation after their first baby, and he discovered the second boy was not his. He felt rejected, lonely and became lost in an alcoholic depression that almost finished him.

He held Vanessa's hand and then kissed her cheek. She smiled, and he moved close to feel her warmth. She was the reason for his new focus in life, and he could not let her down. He looked through the window and noticed a rainbow arc peeking round the edge of the curtain.

'Well, maybe I do have a low sperm count,' he said and threw the magazine to the foot of the bed. 'It might mean IVF and that could be expensive.'

Brian was standing at the window, watching the people in the street as they struggled with their umbrellas against the wind and rain. Mike came into his office.

'Where have you been? You should have been at the meeting. We discussed the 'in house' software option.'

'I had a doctor's appointment,' Brian said. 'I need a favour.'

Brian explained that a vasectomy reversal was not a guaranteed success. Doctor Chambers preferred 'intro-cytoplasmic sperm injection', removing the sperm with a needle and then using in vitro fertilisation. This had the advantage of not interfering with the present state of the vas deferens and there would be no need of a reverse of the reversal later when the children were born.

'Sounds positive,' Mike said and waited for the reason behind Brain's stomach-churning explanation.

'It's expensive, up to five thousand pounds each time. It might not work.' Brain turned to him. 'Doctor Chambers suggested that using a donor would be the less expensive and a painless option. Mike, I would like you to consider—'

'No Brain. No, no, no. I thought they used anonymous donors. Brian, no.'

'The house is mortgaged, and I am paying maintenance to Susan. I just can't afford it. What am I to tell Vanessa?'

The toddler giggled. His blond hair ruffled in the breeze as he ran behind Toby on the lawn with both hands holding the dog's tail. Agnes sat on the patio and watched him as she turned the pages of the photo album on her lap, comparing pictures of her twins to the laughing boy.

'All children look the same as toddlers,' said Mike. He scrubbed hard with the small wire brush to clean the dirt from the groves of his pitching iron.

The garden gate squeaked, and Brian rushed around the corner.

'Daddy, look,' shouted the toddler as he ran after Toby.

'Well!' said Agnes and Mike.

'A baby girl! Six pounds, three ounces,' Brian shouted. 'Hi Callum,' he called to the toddler. ' You have a baby sister. Annabelle.'

'Vanessa is fine, delighted, so happy,' Brian answered Agnes's silent stare.

'Congratulations.' Mike shook his hand.

'Vanessa is so happy.' Brian took a deep breath and bear-hugged Mike. 'Thank you so much. They are worth every single penny I owe you.' A tear rolled down his face as he watched Callum racing after Toby on the lawn.

Harvey's Bistro

'You may kiss the bride.'

Douglas leaned over and kissed Laura before she saw his tears. He glanced away; he swallowed the moisture at the back of his throat.

After a deep breath, he whispered. 'So, Laura Marina Kempinski, you are Mrs Harvey now.'

She grinned and, with a handkerchief, wiped the tears from his cheek. They turned and faced the guests.

Mother's hat feather hung limp, and she held a tissue over her nose. When she had come into the church, she kept on asking Douglas what religion the grandchildren would be. As if that was all she worried about.

Laura's father was frowning. He fidgeted with his gold watch, its chain dangling from the waistcoat pocket of his Higgins and Brown suit. The exchange of wedding vows had not taken very long. Still, he checked the time and shuffled around in his seat. With his broken nose and suave suit, he could easily be mistaken as "Morzeny", in the Bond film, *"From Russia with Love"*.

Douglas saw his mother blow her feather to one side, and she gave a hesitant wave. She dropped her tissue onto the pile by her feet on the floor. He had been desperate for money, and she knew how this wedding conveniently solved all his problems.

Last year, the idea of marriage had never occurred to Douglas. He had sat up in bed, punched his pillows and closed his eyes. Rising from a penniless chef to owning Harvey's Bistro was his ambition. He could see it all in his dream; the customers sat at the tables, busy office girls with sandwiches for lunch, afternoon shoppers having coffee and cake, and in the evening the champagne bubbles would glitter in the candlelight as happy couples made eternal promises.

Trained by the Army Catering Corps as a Master Chef, he had often been called into the banquet hall where the Generals applauded him for the Michelin star service of their formal functions.

Mother had been so full of laughter when she signed the second mortgage for the house to buy the cafe. It's in the high street she had kept telling all her friends at church.

A gust of wind had rattled the slates on the roof, and he sprang out of bed to close the window as the rain thrashed against the panes.

He pulled the duvet up and shivered. The fluorescent numbers from the alarm clock illuminated the café keys on the bedside table. The staff in Donaldson & Co had dangled them ceremoniously as he took possession of them. Everyone had shaken his hand, clinked wine glasses and wished him lots of good luck with his enterprise.

So, what. He didn't even know which key opened the café door. The flames had shot out from the shattered windows and the fire roared up the front of the café façade. In the crowd, schoolboys had clapped and yelled instructions to the firefighters on the platform ladder directing water. On the other side of the street he had gasped for breath, stumbled around the ally, beside the Canton restaurant and retched up bitter bile over his shoes.

He didn't get to start the business and although the firefighters saved the adjacent shop; they let his café burn. His plans for Harvey's Bistro were now a pile of rubble and ash.

The Norwich Union letter was adamant; "Dear Mr Harvey, the fire investigations and report are essential before we will consider any amount as an insurance payout."

It will be fine mother had said when she ironed his shirt and trousers. She hung them with the blazer and his regimental tie behind the bedroom door. Tomorrow, that nice Peter Whelan, he'll know what to do. He does readings for us on Sundays. It's not the end of the world, she had said. Optimistically, she believed in prayer and after bad comes good luck.

He slipped further under the duvet. If only he could get warm, if only he was somewhere else, if only the wind would ease rattling the slates and let him sleep.

Douglas stood inside the reception office and looked around at the refurbished décor and new furniture. There was a pleasant smell of fresh lavender and a faint odour of percolating coffee.

'Come in. Please take a seat.' The receptionist pointed. 'Mr Whelan will call. When he's ready.'

He eased the knot on his Gurkha Brigade tie. The receptionist was new. Smart looking, about five-ten, mid-twenties, and had her red hair pulled back into a bun. Her green tights, short tweed skirt and her white cotton blouse were fresh and neat. She caught him staring and smiled. She pointed again to the seats. There was a sparkle in her grey-green eyes before she turned to face the computer on the desk.

The blazer was rubbing where the barber had shaved his neck' and he ran his fingers under the collar. From his position in the corner, he had a clear view of the girl working with her keyboard. Maybe afterwards, he would ask her if she enjoyed the cinema. There was the new *Sixth Sense* film being screened, and everyone was raving about it.

He looked through the *Times* newspaper and the magazines lying on the occasional table. Mr Whelan was taking his time. The receptionist's typing clacked on her keyboard and the electric clock on the wall hummed.

He stood up, adjusted his tie, and opened the top button of his shirt. He stretched his arms, walked over to the window, and looked out. Damn! He rapped on the glass. The traffic warden smiled back at him and slipped a parking ticket under the wiper of his van, then shuffled off.

The typing stopped. He turned and saw the receptionist rummage through her handbag. She tipped the contents onto the desk. Her purse bounced and slid across the floor to his feet. He picked it up. She ran out from behind the desk and grabbed hold of it.

'Thank you,' she said.

'Has he forgotten?' Douglas held on.

She pulled the purse, but he tightened his grip. She twisted her grip. He pulled back.

'Yutz,' she said, 'I'll buzz him.' She pressed a key on the desk intercom with her free hand.

'Ok. Thank you.' He let go of her leather pouch.

The door to the adjoining office opened and a short, wry-faced man strode through. He wore a dark suit, blue-striped shirt and a purple tie.

'Hallo there. Ah, Mr Harvey. Glad you could make it. Please go on in.'

Douglas reached out for a handshake, but Whelan ignored the gesture and walked past to his receptionist.

'Laura, call Edinburgh. My wife will come along after all.' He turned and directed Douglas into his office.

'Well now, please sit down, Mr Harvey.' Whelan pulled at his shirt cuffs and went behind his desk. 'There, this won't take long.' He smiled. 'I expect you're a busy man.'

'Aye right, we've got all morning.' Douglas sat back in the chair.

'Yes, well.' Whelan grinned. 'The good news is we received a letter from Norwich Union.'

'Great stuff. I'd not heard anything.' He sat up. 'Does that mean I can go ahead?'

'Steady on there, not yet.' Whelan brushed his hand through his grey hair. 'How's your mother?

'How do you expect? She's a nervous wreck.' Douglas slid forward on the leather seat. 'What do you mean, not yet?'

'Well, the fire report says definite arson. And yes, well. It's still under investigation.'

'How long will—'

'Mr Harvey, it could be months or even years. It's a complicated affair.' He shuffled the letters on his desk and put on his glasses. 'Well, there's the previous owner, and he's claimed on his insurance and there's a suggestion of a collusion and fraud.'

'But surely, he can't do that. Can he?'

'Yes, well. Look, you'll be happy to know we've renegotiated the loan to an interest only arrangement for you.' He peered over his glasses. 'Interest only for six months. The Norwich Union has assured me this should be sufficient time for them to resolve the issue.'

'What then?'

'Then, Mr Harvey?' Whelan removed his glasses and sat back in his chair. 'I see what you mean after six months. Yes, the Bank may consider selling 8 Orchard Way, Mr Harvey.' Whelan licked at his top lip.

'It's my mother's house.'

'Ah yes, your mother's house.' He put the letters back into a folder. 'But not to worry, it's a lovely house, with an extensive garden. The nearby school might encourage a quick sale.' He threw the folder onto his out tray.

There were two loud knocks on the door, and the receptionist rushed into the office.

'Excuse me, Mr Whelan. Your wife has arrived.'

'There you have it, Mr Harvey, six months. Laura will show you out.'

'Sir, no, please.' Douglas stood up. 'I'm not selling the house.'

Laura raised her voice. 'Mr Whelan, your wife is waiting.'

'Tell your mother I said Hallo.' Mr Whelan strode out.

Douglas sat down and put his head in his hands.

'Mr Harvey, you need to leave.' She held the door open.

'It's my mother's home.' He got up and left Whelan's office. 'What am I to tell her?'

'Would you like a coffee, Mr Harvey?' She walked past him, her heels tapping on the parquet floor. 'It's fresh, you'll feel better.'

'Feel better. I'm losing my home and my dream. All gone.' He took the cup from Laura and slowly sipped the milky coffee. 'Can I have some sugar? Please.'

I've read the file, Mr Harvey. It's a shame. Really.' She put her hand on his shoulder and slid it down his arm to his elbow. She gave it a reassuring squeeze. 'What are you going to do, Mr Harvey?' She stepped away and sat on her desk.

He could smell the herbal shampoo from her hair and lowered his head.

'Please, call me Douglas. I don't want to talk about it.'

'The insurance will pay up, eventually. That's what Mr Whelan told me.'

'Aye, but I still need to find the interest until then.'

'O yes, the interest. I know someone who might help.'

'Aye now, who would that be?'

'My father might. Why not ask him?' She searched around in her handbag.

'Is he rich or something?'

'Have you heard of the Kempinski Hotel and Country Club?' She pulled her mobile from the bag.

'Who? No, not really.' He sat down. Everyone knows the rumours about Kempinski, and how he had threatened customers in his garage with an axe. They call him "Leo the Hatchet, the mechanic who fixes things". But then again, anyone with a flash BMW around here is probably a gangster. 'Can we not talk about this?'

'What about your dream? I wish I had your ambition.'

'Everyone's got ambitions, but maybe not the money.'

'I'll speak to my father about your bistro. Give me your number. I'll call later.'

'Ah, tell you what. Do you like the cinema? The *Sixth Sense* is on in Hamilton.'

She went behind her desk and sat down.

'How about it? I'll tell you all about my ambitions.' He smiled.

Douglas arrived at the Country club.

After missing three interest payments, Laura had convinced him that her father's help was the best option. He knows what it's like to dream; she had said, look how well he has done. Forget the rumours.

'Mr Kempinski,' he called and went up to the man sitting on the veranda.

Leo, at sixty-four, had the hard muscular stature of a boxer. He was sitting alone and was staring across the lawn towards the fairways. He held a cassette player in his lap and wore a checked pullover.

'Ah, Douglas.' He took out the earphones. 'Dimtri Shostakovich Piano Trio. It makes me weep.' His smile connected with the scar on the left side of his face. 'De coffee, please.'

Douglas filled two cups from the thermos and sat down. Laura had advised him to let her father do the talking; it saves a lot of time, and don't wear your army tie, he hates soldiers.

'You see, Douglas, de café maybe a wonderful investment with forty percent help from Mr Taxman for de Venture Capital,' Leo said. 'Sounds too simple, maybe, no?'

'And ten percent profits.' Douglas nodded.

'No, no, we will be family. Yes, of course, de fire insurance money.' He chuckled. 'Laura, she is a smart girl. What do you think?'

'Yes.' Douglas nodded.

'See de tree?' Leo said. 'Is maybe two hundred years old.' He pointed to the large oak in the middle of the lawn. Leo took a picture from his bag and passed it over.

'De tree trunk is like a village, each year a little bigger.' Leo said. 'Every generation growing de next.'

Douglas turned the picture away from the glare of the sun. It was of Laura and her mother laughing by the same tree where they were holding a birthday cake with candles.

'We counted many generations.' Leo pointed at the picture. 'All in Kempinski's family book. They burned to nothing.' He thumped the table and knocked his coffee over.

Douglas sat up and looked away.

'The Einsatzgrüppen, dey come to my village, Jedwabne. Run Leon run, my mother, she screams. I see dem in our village burn everybody in de synagogue.'

Laura had the same nose and cheeks as her mother's, in the photograph. They were both beautiful.

'We live in de forest. But all family gone.' Leo stared at him. 'Children are like acorns. You listening? Do you understand what I mean? Douglas?'

'I think so.'

The air was warming, and wisps of mist rose along the fairways. Douglas squinted in the sunshine and tipped his head to see Leo's face.

'Mr Kempinski, you have a bonny daughter.'

'You do not say, she is bonny.' Leo laughed and thumped Douglas on the shoulder. 'I know. Tell me, you like her.' He sat forward and poked Douglas's chest. 'Be careful. She is a very stubborn woman.'

'I like her very much.' He put the picture on the table and looked away.

'I hope she likes you very much, too. Are you ready? Aah.' Leo stood up. 'Maybe I think yes.'

Two BMW Estates drove past the veranda into the car park and stopped by the golf buggies.

'If you love her,' Leo said and gripped him on the shoulder. 'First, make me a lucky man. Afterwards, we arrange the money for the café.' He picked up his golf bag and walked off to meet his friends. He shouted back, 'If you love her, make me happy.'

The group loaded their bags into a golf cart and drove to the first tee. They each struck a ball down the fairway towards the distant green, its red flag protruding above a bowl of mist.

Douglas rubbed his bruised shoulder. Instead of a loan, Leo had left him a photograph. If you love her, first make me happy, he had said.

He tapped out a text on his phone; "Ok, will come riding. C U". He threw the cold coffee from his cup out over the lawn, picked up the picture and walked to his van behind the hedge.

The agreement was with Laura. She would convince her father to finance the bistro and she wanted seventy-five percent of the insurance money but settled on fifty. Had Leo expected him to talk about getting married, was that the condition for his money?

He swiped away the spider's web from the van's wing mirror. Three attempts later, the engine started, and he drove past the cars at the clubhouse. Someday soon he'll have a BMW. He pushed a CD into the player and sung along. "Well, this is just between us ..."

Douglas kept a grip on the saddle to steady himself on the horse. This wasn't as easy as he expected. What if he fell? Whenever he moved to get comfortable, the grey mare snorted, swept her tail and stomped around before she settled. In front of him, on the chestnut stallion, he saw how relaxed Laura sat. She was in control and rode with a coordinated rhythm to the horse's gait.

She looked back and called. 'Are you okay?'

He nodded. 'Aye, I'm fine.'

'Come on then, let's give the horses a run.' She urged the stallion into a gallop across the open ground.

The mare leapt forward, and Douglas's backside hit the saddle hard, causing him to bite his bottom lip. He grasped at the reins to stop from falling and stood in the stirrups like a jockey at Ascot. It was exhilarating to gallop across the field, but could he trust the mare not to throw him? He spat blood into the air.

Laura stood in the stirrups with her knees tight against her saddle, her jodhpurs stretched tight. It looked so easy the way she turned the stallion and rode on towards a barn.

His horse veered in the opposite direction towards the boundary fence and a low gate. He pulled frantically on the reins and held tight. If this horse jumps, he might fall and his broken bones wouldn't be as painful as the humiliation of lying in the hospital. Then where would he be with his bistro? The mare pulled and stretched against the reins and kept its course.

He heard Laura's whistles and calls, and the mare's ears shifted about. The horse slowed to a trot, turning towards the barn. Laura had dismounted and waved her whip in the air. The mare walked forward, snorted and stomped until Laura grabbed the bridle and tied the reins to a post.

'Wahoo, that was great.' He slid off the saddle.

She struck his legs with the crop. 'You said you could ride, you idiot.'

'That hurt.' He grabbed at the whip but missed. 'Look, I said I've done some pony trekking.'

'Yutz, you could've fallen.' She removed her gloves and pulled a tissue from her jacket pocket. 'You're bleeding, let me.' She wiped at his split lip. 'You could have died.'

He pulled off his scull helmet. 'Killed? Not not me.'

'That's what you think.' She took hold of his hand and led him into the barn.

'Listen, you know your father hasn't agreed to arrange the money yet.'

'He told me De Café Kempinski is okay.' She pulled him towards her and kissed him. 'Tell me later,' she said, and they rolled over onto the hay bales.

'He expects the insurance money to cover the loan.' He sat up. 'What do you mean, de café Kempinski?'

'You worry too much.' She touched his nose. 'Come on, pull my boots off.'

Douglas buttoned his shirt and searched for his trousers. Laura had dressed and adjusted her helmet.

'Your father kept on about the oak tree.' He slipped on his jacket.

'Shmaltzy. He is a sentimental yutz.' She threw his boots across to him. 'He says, "it's duty to have children. For the family", blah.' She sat down on the hay. 'You think he gives me everything?' She picked up the crop. 'Well, I have nothing. It all belongs to him. I belong to him. But when I have my money, it will be different.'

'You know I can't afford to pay the bank interest and your father's loan.'

'Maybe he thinks he is giving me the money for the café.'

'So that's it. I'm to make him a happy man just for the money.'

'You're a yutz.' She swiped her crop at the hay bales. 'Stick your bloody insurance money.' She got up and walked towards the horses.

'Twenty minutes ago, you loved me,' he called. 'You'd do anything. Was that just for the money?'

She turned back into the barn. 'Yes, maybe it was.' She lifted the crop to his nose. 'I'm sorry. But I won't marry just to please my father.'

'Be my business partner, we'll run the Bistro together.'

'No Douglas.'

He grabbed her jacket collar, twisted his arm around her neck, and pulled her close to his face. 'Now listen to me, you poor little rich madam.'

'That hurts, Doug. Let me go.'

'Sorry.' He let her go. 'Okay, it wasn't the plan. But you know I love you more than your father's money.' He let her go and took a small box from his pocket. 'I bought this ages ago.' He took out the ring. 'I was thinking I'd open the bistro first. Laura Kempinski will.'

'Business partners and one hundred percent.'

'Yes Laura, one hundred percent commitment.'

'Then yes. I will Douglas Harvey.' She grabbed his face with both hands and kissed him.

'You'll still have to ask my father,' she said.

It was early evening as they walked back through the woods, where the trees muffled the sounds of the horses' hooves and the occasional rustle of blackbirds foraging in the undergrowth.

'My grandparents died in the woods,' she said. 'My father still cries when he tells the story.'

Douglas shivered. The movement of the clouds formed shadows that crept amongst the trees, as if the Kempinski's ghosts had risen from their forest graves.

At the stables, Douglas saw Leo come out from the office into the courtyard. Laura rushed forward, kissed her father on the cheek, and whispered in his ear. They glanced back at him, nodded, smiled and laughed.

'You make me a happy man.' Leo offered his arms wide open and hugged him. 'Laura, take the horses. Douglas wants to talk.'

'Mr Kempinski I—'

'Please, I am Leo. We are family.' He was laughing and shook Douglas by the shoulders. 'Now we grow family. We grow Café Kempinski and—'

'Harvey's Bistro. It's my business.'

'Schmutze, what are you say.' Leo slapped him on his shoulder. 'You like Witz. What about the problem? No, no, it is family. We call it Café Kempinski. Yes?'

'Mr Kempinski, I appreciate your offer to help, but it must be my business.'

'No, no, is present for Laura, our Café Kempinski.'

'It has to be Harvey's Bistro. My café or nothing.'

'What about mother? Laura says Whelan wants your mother's house.'

'Mr Kempinski, do you want to see my mother homeless? In the forest?'

'Schmutze, what are you say.' Leo punched him hard on the helmet. 'You know nothing about the forest. Go home. Go home to mother.'

Douglas threw the scull-hat across the stable yard and stomped to his van. It started the first time. In his mirror, he saw Laura chase after him as he drove out onto the main road.

Fresh cut grass has a sweet smell that compliments the taste of Glenmorangie, especially on a warm afternoon. The borders were neat, cleared of weeds, and he had watered the petunia and marigolds. Mother would be pleased when she gets back from church. Douglas sat back and tilted his face towards the sun. He closed his eyes.

He was a fool. A 'Yutz' Laura had called him. She cried, then called him an idiot. Perhaps it's her lifestyle she can't let go, trapped by money if anyone believes her. Leo wanted Café Kempinski for Laura as the centre of his *'alla polacca'* and the idea of village life. With them, it would never be Harvey's Bistro.

A movement in the garden distracted him.

'Laura.' He said and jumped to his feet.

'Congratulations, I see the renovation work has started.'

'The Norwich agreed to pay, as you said.'

'I know.' She took off her sunglasses. 'Whelan is furious. I can see why. This is a lovely house.'

'You are looking well, you know we could—'

'Please Douglas, don't. I was just passing.'

He followed her out to the lane, and she got into her Audi Sports cabriolet.

'A birthday present.' she said and fiddled with a CD.

'Why don't you come and see the café?' He held on to the top of the driver's door.

'Oh, I will, when it's finished.' She looked up at him. 'Kiss me, Douglas.'

'Only, if you promise to be my business partner, seriously.'

'I'll think about it.' She slowly drove off and shouted back. 'Maybe I will, I promise.'

He heard the volume on the music system turn up louder and he heard the words, "I hope you miss me, put me down on history."

The Cranberries-Bury the Hatchet. 'Loud and Clear'.

Books by James McEwan

The Listener Anthology of Short Stories

ISBN 978-1-508938-97-2

Missing (A Psychological Novel)

ISBN 978-1-913202-00-02

Russell Holmes Investigates.

Short Stories of

Murder

ISBN 978-1-913202-01-9

Flash Fiction Blog

jplmcewan.wordpress.com

Printed in Dunstable, United Kingdom

68471292R00058